Sendi Lee Mason

AND THE STRAY STRIPED CAT

Sendi Lee Mason

AND THE
STRAY STRIPED CAT

Hilda Stahl

CROSSWAY BOOKS • WHEATON, ILLINOIS 60187
A DIVISION OF GOOD NEWS PUBLISHERS

Sendi Lee Mason and the Stray Striped Cat.

Copyright © 1990 by Hilda Stahl.

Published by Crossway Books, a division of
Good News Publishers, Wheaton, Illinois 60187.

Cover design: Ad Plus

Cover illustration: Deborah Huffman

First printing, 1990
Second printing, 1991

Printed in the United States of America

Library of Congress Catalog Card Number 90-80621

ISBN 0-89107-580-1

Dedicated with love to
Evangelynn Kaye

Contents

1

The Stray Cat

Sendi raced down the sidewalk with Diane
close behind. Sweat soaked Sendi's stained
yellow tee shirt and dampened her blonde
shoulder-length hair. The sun was already
blazing hot even this early in the morning.

"You can't get away from me, Sendi
Mason!" shouted Diane Roscommon.

"Leave me alone!" cried Sendi.

"Tell me what you're looking for!"

called Diane. She always wanted to know everything that was going on.

Sendi ran faster, dodged around some bushes, and then ducked around the corner of her house. She didn't dare let Diane know about the cat, or Diane would scare him away.

Sendi's thin chest rose and fell. Smells of bacon drifted across the street. A car honked from the busy street two blocks away. She peered around her house to see if Diane had spotted her. "She's gone," she whispered in relief.

Just then Sendi caught a movement in the bushes that separated her yard from the Hansens'. She held her breath and waited. The huge gray and black striped stray cat walked out from under the bushes. He stopped and watched a bird fly to a low branch.

Sendi's breath caught in her throat as she studied the wonderful, big ugly cat. Part of his right ear was missing, and a piece of hide was torn off his right shoulder. Oh, but she wanted the cat to learn to trust her and love her!

"I want you to be my cat," whispered Sendi, standing as still as she could. The cat was bigger than Gwen's long-haired white cat, Camille, and he looked hungry and scared. Sendi felt sorry for him. She knew just how he felt. She wasn't hungry all the time, but she was scared a lot because she had to stay home alone all day while Mom worked. Styling hair at Hair Care didn't earn enough to pay a baby-sitter.

Sendi glanced at Gwen's house next door. Unlike the dry, brown grass in Sendi's yard, Gwen's lawn was bright green and pretty because of the water sprinkler going most of the day. Gwen hadn't come out yet this morning.

If Gwen walked out of her house right now, she would probably chase the stray cat away, Sendi thought. Gwen wouldn't want the stray cat to fight with Camille.

"My cat won't hurt Camille," whispered

Sendi as the big cat batted a moth and ate it. Sendi screwed up her face and tried not to get sick to her stomach. It was awful to think her cat was forced to eat moths. She wanted to feed him cat food from a can and milk from a bowl.

Just then the cat streaked away and disappeared in the bushes behind Gwen's house. Sendi dashed after him. Up ahead she saw him duck under a bush two houses beyond Gwen's. Sendi stopped in the yard and dropped down on her stomach. She inched forward toward the bush where she'd seen the cat hide. Dried grass tickled Sendi's chin, and a twig dug into her stomach through her tee shirt. The hot August sun burned down on her blonde head. "Here, kitty," she called softly.

"He's not there now," said a man behind Sendi.

Sendi leaped up with a frightened shriek. She stared at the old man's dusty cowboy boots, faded jeans, and blue plaid cotton shirt — up to the wide-brimmed cowboy hat that shaded his rugged, sun-browned face. She glanced around to see if anyone was in sight to help her in case the man was bad. They were all alone. She locked her icy hands together. She knew she should run away, but she didn't want to leave the cat. "You're a stranger! I can't talk to you," she said, backing away.

The man grinned, and Sendi saw that one of his front teeth had a tiny corner chipped off. "I'm Pine Cordell, and I just moved in here last night." He stabbed a thumb toward the small house. "I won't hurt you none."

Sendi glanced at the house. The same white curtains hung at the window as when Pete, who was really a missing child named Isaac, and his dad had lived there. An old beat-up red pickup stood in the short driveway. Finally Sendi looked back at Pine Cordell. "Is the cat yours?"

"Nope." Pine pushed his hat to the back of his head. Gray wisps of hair stood up above his ears. Wrinkles fanned out from the corners of his bright blue eyes to his hairline. "Looks to me like an old stray tomcat that's been in plenty of battles. I was watching him earlier this morning. His right ear is half gone."

"I know." Sendi rubbed her hand over her yellow tee shirt and down her dusty yellow shorts. "When I first walked outside this morning, I saw the cat watching a bird. He looked hungry and tired, and I wanted to catch him and feed him." And she'd wanted him to be her pet, but she didn't tell the old cowboy that.

"Do you live near here?" asked Pine, peering down at Sendi. She nodded and pointed. "Two houses down, in the smallest house on the block."

Pine narrowed his eyes and looked to where she was pointing. "And what's your name?"

"Sendi Lee Mason." She moved from one sneaker to the other. Should she run away from Pine Cordell or keep talking to him? She decided to keep talking. "I'm nine, and I'll be in fourth grade when school starts next week." She glanced up questioningly at Pine Cordell. "Do you have kids for me to play with?"

Pine chuckled and shook his head. "My kids are growed, but I got grandkids and even a couple of great-grandkids. I just moved here from a ranch in Wyoming to be near my youngest girl and her family."

"Do they live on this block?" asked Sendi.

"Nope. On the other side of the park." Pine looped his thumbs in his belt. "When you're at the park sometime, I'll introduce you to them if you want."

"Okay," said Sendi.

Just then the big cat ambled around the house and stopped in front of the battered red pickup.

"Do you want to tame that wild critter?" asked Pine.

"Yes," said Sendi just above a whisper.

"Then you got to give him plenty of rope," said Pine.

Sendi frowned at him. "What rope?"

Pine chuckled. "That's cowboy talk. It means, don't make him feel closed in. He don't look like he wants to belong to anybody. But that could be only his way to keep from getting hurt." Pine nodded while the cat sat on his haunches and licked his shoulder with a small pink tongue. "People have a way of doing that too. They act like they don't need anybody, but inside they're hurting for love and attention."

Sendi kept her eyes glued to the cat. She acted that way a lot, especially with Gwen's mom and dad. She didn't want them to guess that she'd love to have parents like them. They were gone a lot doing important things, but when they were around, they hugged and kissed Gwen and gave her things that she didn't even ask for.

Pine squatted down and held out his hand. "Here, kitty. Here, kitty. I won't hurt you."

Sendi held her breath and waited, but the cat turned slowly and walked away. "I wish he'd come to me," she said.

"Feed him at your back door every morning. Before you know it, you'll have a friend," said Pine. "But don't try to touch him until he comes right up to you, or you'll scare him away."

Sendi nodded. She'd feed the cat, but she wouldn't touch him. And Gwen and Diane had better not try to stop her!

2

Gwen

Sendi ran around her house and stopped short. Gwen stood at the back door with a scowl on her usually smiling face. She spun around to face Sendi.

"Sendi!" Gwen cried. "I need you!"

"Why?" asked Sendi. Was Gwen hunting for another missing child? She wanted to tell Gwen she had work to do, but she didn't want her to get suspicious. And she couldn't tell Gwen about the cat.

Gwen squared her shoulders and flipped her long brown hair back. Her brown eyes sparkled. "I have major work to do! And I desperately need your help!"

Sendi frowned. She didn't want to get involved in Gwen's major work. "There aren't any missing kids around here, Gwen. You already checked up on all of them."

Laughing, Gwen flung out her arms. "Finding missing kids is only one of my goals in life, Sendi."

"Oh," said Sendi in a tiny voice.

"My main goal now is to get all the kids in our neighborhood to say NO to drugs!" Gwen stepped right up to Sendi. "Let me hear you say it."

"Say what?" asked Sendi.

"NO!"

Sendi looked puzzled.

Gwen pushed her nose almost against Sendi's. "You don't do drugs, do you, Sendi?" she asked in alarm.

"No! I'd never do drugs!"

"Then let me hear you say no to drugs. Come on. Say it," said Gwen. She sighed heavily. "Please, Sendi. As my very best friend, will you say it? If I can't even get you to say it, how will I get anyone else to?"

Sendi sighed loud and long. "Okay. NO to drugs!"

Gwen beamed and patted Sendi on the back. "Thank you. You are a good friend."

Sendi looked around quickly to make sure no one had heard her and thought she was dumb. Nobody was in sight. She turned back to Gwen. "I gotta go now."

"You do?" Gwen tilted her head and studied Sendi. "Is Diane forcing you to play with her again?"

"No," said Sendi.

"Then come with me to get all the kids to say no to drugs."

Sendi didn't want to say anything that would hurt Gwen, but she couldn't tell her that she was going to get food for the stray cat. "I have things to do," Sendi finally said.

Gwen's shoulders slumped. "Anyone who does great deeds leads a very lonely life."

Just then the Hansen boys ran out into their backyard, shouting and wrestling as usual. Sendi pointed to them. "Go ask the Hansen boys to help you."

Gwen rolled her eyes. "You know they won't. They think I'm weird."

Sendi nodded. She'd become friends with Gwen for that very reason. Gwen was the first weird person Sendi had ever met. Sendi bit her bottom lip. As long as she could remember, people had called Sendi weird. Until she moved here, she and Mom had lived with Momma. Momma was really Sendi's grandma, but she'd always called her Momma like Mom did. Kids always made fun of Sendi for doing that. And Sendi had no dad. The kids said she was probably some kind of alien. But she knew she wasn't, and she had a birth certificate to prove it. Being called weird was nothing new to Sendi.

"Please, Sendi," begged Gwen with her hands clasped under her chin and her pleading brown eyes wide. "I need you."

Sendi sighed heavily. "All right," she

said. She'd have to feed the cat later when Gwen wasn't around.

Gwen jumped up and down and shouted, "You won't be sorry, Sendi. You'll feel so good about helping me that you'll want to do it every day." Suddenly she squared her shoulders and grew very serious. She pulled her pink tee shirt down over her blue shorts. "We'll start my major work with the Hansen boys!"

Sendi hung back, but Gwen grabbed her arm and tugged her through the break in the hedges and into the Hansens' backyard.

Shawn, Teddy, and Bruce looked up at the girls. "Did you come to see if we are missing kids?" asked Shawn, the oldest. He laughed and jabbed his brothers. They jabbed him back. They looked alike with dark hair and eyes. Their shorts and white tee shirts hung on their thin bodies.

Sendi bit back an embarrassed giggle. She'd been with Gwen when she'd accused two kids of being missing children, only to discover that they weren't.

Gwen flipped back her dark hair and stepped right up to the boys. "You won't make fun of my new mission in life!"

"What is it?" asked Shawn with a laugh.

"I am getting all the kids in the neighborhood to say no to drugs." Gwen looked excitedly at each boy. "So, say it."

"Say what?" asked Bruce, the seven-year-old.

"Repeat after me," said Sendi to make it easier for the boys. She wanted to finish the job so she could get back to her cat. "Ready?" She waited until the boys nodded. She held up both hands as if leading a choir, and then waved them as she said, "NO to drugs!"

"NO to drugs!" the boys shouted as loudly as they could. Then they leaped on each other and fell to the ground in a laughing heap.

"There," said Gwen. She brushed her hands together and smiled. "Mission accomplished at the Hansens'. Now, let's go to the Roscommons'. That will be quite a challenge."

"Especially if their mom won't let them come outdoors yet," said Sendi. She really didn't want to face Diane and have her ask why she'd run from her a while ago.

Gwen lifted her arm high and shouted, "No door will bar me from my mission! Let's go!"

Sendi glanced around for her cat. He wasn't in sight. She sighed and ran after Gwen to the house next door. Diane had two younger sisters and two older brothers. Since she was the middle child, Diane said she felt like a thin layer of peanut butter smashed between two thick slices of bread.

Gwen waited for Sendi, and then knocked on the back door. Mrs. Roscommon answered it.

"The kids are cleaning their rooms and will be out later," Mrs. Roscommon said.

Sendi expected Gwen to push right on in, but she nodded and slowly turned away.

Just then Sendi saw the stray cat amble into sight. Sendi turned Gwen around before she could see the cat. "Gwen, did you know someone new moved into the house down the block?"

"No! Who is it?" asked Gwen excitedly. "Maybe I'll find another missing child, and maybe I can get him to say no to drugs!"

Sendi shook her head. "It's a man named Pine Cordell, and he's a cowboy."

"Pine? What kind of name is that?" asked Gwen.

"His name," said Sendi. "I met him this morning. He's nice, and he might be able to give you some help on your mission against drugs."

"Why? Does he do drugs?" asked Gwen with her eyes narrowed.

"Go ask him while I run home for a while," said Sendi, trying to push Gwen on her way.

Just then Camille walked into sight. She meowed at the stray cat.

Sendi froze.

Gwen turned around and saw Camille, and then saw the stray cat. She ran at the stray cat with a loud yell. The stray cat streaked away.

Sendi leaped after Gwen and caught her, but it was too late. The cat was gone and maybe wouldn't come back again. Sendi pushed Gwen hard, and she fell to the grass.

"Sendi!" cried Gwen in surprise. "Why did you push me down?"

Sendi closed her mouth tightly and knotted her fists at her sides.

Slowly Gwen stood up. "Were you being mean to me, Sendi?" asked Gwen in a small, hurt voice.

Sendi blinked back hot, stinging tears. "I am not going to help you with your mission, Gwen McNeeley! I'm going home right now!"

"But why?" asked Gwen.

Sendi narrowed her eyes. "I don't want to be friends with anyone who chases away hungry animals! So there!"

"But he'd hurt Camille." Gwen scooped the big white cat up in her arms and looked over her head at Sendi. "Camille is my pet, and that cat is an ugly stray!"

Tears burning her eyes, Sendi whirled around and ran next door to her yard. What if the stray cat never came back again?

"Don't be angry, Sendi!" Gwen ran to Sendi's yard. "Please don't be angry."

"Leave me alone," snapped Sendi.

Camille squirmed, and Gwen let her leap to the ground. She walked to a bright patch of sun and carefully washed herself.

Gwen's lip quivered. "We're best friends, Sendi. Best friends don't want to be left alone."

"I don't like you," said Sendi. The terrible words stabbed into her heart, but she didn't take them back.

Gwen's face turned red, then white. "But I like you!"

"Get out of my yard!" Sendi pushed Gwen, and she stumbled back and almost fell over. She burst into tears and ran home.

Sendi walked slowly to her back door.

She didn't need a best friend, especially
not one who chased away a wonderful
stray striped cat who needed love and food
and had only half a right ear.

3

The Cat Collar

Sendi slowly ate her bologna sandwich and her ice cream bar. Then she sat with her elbows on the table and her chin in her hands. "The cat didn't come again this morning. Maybe he won't this afternoon either," she said with a catch in her voice.

Maybe she should find Gwen and tell her she was sorry and see if she wanted to play in the park for a while. She'd been really bad to Gwen. Tears burned the backs of Sendi's eyes. Should she tell Gwen that she was really, really sorry for pushing her down and for yelling at her?

Before Sendi could move, someone knocked at the back door. She ran to answer it. Gwen stood there, her eyes puffy and red from crying. Sendi wanted to hug Gwen hard and say she was sorry, but somehow she couldn't. Her family didn't hug or kiss like Gwen's family.

"Can I come in?" Gwen asked, sniffling.

Sendi couldn't talk around the lump in her throat, so she stepped aside and waited for Gwen to walk in. The door squeaked as she closed it.

Gwen knuckled a tear away as she faced Sendi. "I prayed for a friend, Sendi, and Jesus answered by sending you to me. Jesus is my very best friend, but you are my other best friend."

Sendi's stomach tightened. She had forgotten about Jesus. She knew He didn't want her to be mean to Gwen or to anyone.

He wanted her to love others and be kind. She'd asked Him to be her Friend and Savior, but sometimes she forgot all about Him. It made her feel bad that she could forget such an important person as Jesus. Gwen never seemed to forget Him. But Gwen's parents were Christians too, and they helped Gwen to remember. They always studied their Bibles and went to church together. Sendi only went to church if she woke up in time, and Mom had only gone once since they'd moved here. Neither of them ever read the Bible.

Gwen swallowed hard. "If I did something to make you feel bad, I'm sorry. If you don't want to go with me to get others to say no to drugs, then you don't have to."

Sendi twisted the tail of her tee shirt. She looked down at her dirty sneakers that once had been white and then up at Gwen. "I'll go with you."

"Then why'd you get mad at me?" asked Gwen.

"You . . . chased away the cat," said Sendi in a low, tight voice.

"The stray cat?" asked Gwen in surprise.

Sendi nodded. She took a deep breath and said, "I want the cat as my pet!" She told Gwen how she felt about the cat and how she was going to tame him.

"But what about Camille?" asked Gwen.

"I won't let him hurt Camille," said Sendi.

Gwen narrowed her eyes in thought. "Sendi, in this town every cat that is a pet must wear a collar. Since the stray cat doesn't have a collar, the city will have it picked up or even killed."

Sendi shivered and shook her head hard. "I can't let that happen!"

"Then we must get a collar on your cat. And we have to do it now!" Gwen marched to the door, and then turned. "Are you coming?"

"But I don't have a collar!"

"Oh." Gwen brushed her hair back and thought. "Then we'll just have to get one."

Sendi spread her hands wide. "But I

don't have any money." She didn't want Gwen to know that Mom had said there wasn't even enough money to buy groceries for the week.

"I don't either, but we'll think of something," said Gwen.

"I know!" Sendi ran across the room. "Mom has some stuff we can look through!" She pushed the door open to Mom's room. A hot breeze ruffled the white curtains at the window on the far side of her bed. Smells of perfume and Mom's special smell lingered in the air. The room was neat and tidy. Sendi lifted a shoebox off the shelf in the small closet. She set it on the bed and pulled off the lid. "See?" She showed Gwen the piles of odds and ends of jewelry. "It's stuff that people leave behind at the beauty salon and never come back to claim and stuff Mom bought at yard sales last year. She says someday she'll do something with it. Like make earrings or hair clips or something."

"There's probably something that would work for a cat collar," said Gwen, picking up a long string of red beads. She draped them around her neck, and the beads hung almost to her feet. She giggled and wrapped them around her neck three times until they hung down on her chest the way they were supposed to.

"This looks like a cat collar," said Sendi, holding up a leather strap with diamond-look studs along it.

"It does!" cried Gwen. "We can tape your name and address right along here with that special clear packing tape my dad uses."

Several minutes later Gwen stood in the middle of her parents' study and held the finished collar out to Sendi. "There's your cat collar," Gwen said, smiling.

Sendi took it carefully and held it as if it would break into a million pieces if she dropped it. It was the most beautiful cat collar in the world. Sunlight from the study windows flashed bright colors off the diamond-like studs. Her name and address were easy to read. Gwen had typed them carefully with her mom's typewriter, cut the paper the right size, and taped it in place between the flashing studs.

Sendi walked to the door, and then stopped. "But how will we get the cat to come to us so we can put it on him?"

Gwen frowned. "I never thought of that."

Sendi bit her bottom lip and narrowed her blue eyes. Suddenly she remembered Pine Cordell. "Maybe Pine Cordell can help us! Let's go ask him!"

A few minutes later Sendi stood beside Gwen while they talked to Pine Cordell. He'd been watering his small yard. The hose lay coiled at his feet with a tiny trickle of water oozing out of the nozzle.

"That's a mighty expensive collar to put on a stray cat," said Pine as he ran a thin, brown finger over the diamond-like studs and leather band.

"It's Mom's junk stuff," said Sendi.

"How can we get it on the cat?" asked Gwen.

Pine pushed his hat to the back of his head and narrowed his eyes that looked as blue as the summer sky. "We could set a trap for the cat."

"But not hurt him!" cried Sendi.

"No," said Pine, shaking his head. He

led them inside the garage and showed them a cage that could easily hold the stray. "I'll brace this door open, put food here at the opposite end of the cage, and set it where the cat would see it without getting suspicious. Then when the cat walks in to get the food, the door snaps closed, and the cat is locked inside. But that old cat would be one scared critter."

Sendi thought about the plan for a long time. "I guess it would be better for him to be scared for a while than to be dead. Let's do it."

"And once he's inside, you could slip on the collar," said Gwen, nodding. "That's a wonderful plan."

"You might even want to keep him inside the cage a few days just to show him he can trust you," said Pine.

Sendi smiled. She couldn't wait to be able to touch the cat, pet him, and even hold him the way Gwen held Camille. Soon the stray cat would be hers!

4

Pine's Help

Sendi smiled up at Pine. "Thanks for helping me," she said.

He shrugged and grinned. "Any time, Sendi." He hoisted the cage up on his broad shoulder. "Let's go find the right place for this."

Gwen tucked her hair behind her ears and frowned slightly. "What if Camille sees the bait and walks in the cage?" She'd already told Pine all about herself, her cat, and her great missions in life.

Pine chuckled. "Then we'd just take ole Camille out and set the trap again. That trap can't hurt anything, not even a beauty like Camille."

"Not even if a little kid crawled in there?" asked Sendi, giggling. She knew that would be impossible. The cage was too small for a child.

Pine set the cage under the bushes near his garage. "I'll feel a whole lot better if I take care of our caged animal," he said. "I don't want you girls getting scratched or bit."

"I'll check the cage often," said Sendi. She'd already promised she wouldn't try to put the collar on the cat without Pine's help. "Bye, Pine." He'd told them not to call him Mr. Cordell because nobody ever had, and he didn't want anyone doing it now. Sendi turned to Gwen. "Let's go look for the cat."

Gwen nodded, but didn't move. She touched Pine's arm and said, "I forgot to have you say no to drugs, Pine."

He chuckled. "No to drugs."

Gwen beamed. "I want to get everyone in the neighborhood to say no to drugs."

"That's good, Gwenny," said Pine. "But saying the words is not enough, you know."

Gwen frowned, and Sendi moved restlessly from one foot to the other.

"What do you mean?" asked Gwen.

Sendi rolled her eyes. She knew she couldn't drag Gwen away until she heard what Pine wanted to say.

"Gwen, you want people to stay away from drugs. And that's good," said Pine. He walked to his beat-up old red pickup and leaned against the tailgate while Gwen and Sendi stood in back of it. "You can get everybody to say the words, Gwen, but they need to say them at the right time."

"When is that?" asked Gwen.

Sendi crossed her arms, then dropped them at her sides. She looked up at the puffy white clouds in the sky, then down the street at the blue car just pulling away from the curb. She wanted to look for her cat. She did not want to listen to a lesson on saying no to drugs no matter how important it was.

Pine rubbed a rough hand over his jaw. "My little twelve-year-old grand-daughter Mia is fighting like crazy to stay off drugs. Just saying the words to you wouldn't be enough for her, Gwen. She's got to know why she's saying them, and she's got to know to say them at the right time to the right person." Pine reached out and squeezed Gwen's hand. "So, while you're out getting folks to say no to drugs, you tell them that someday somebody might offer them drugs, and that's the time to say no as loud as they can. And if they don't have the strength to say no by them-selves, tell them to ask the Lord for the strength and the help."

Gwen squared her shoulders, and her eyes flashed with excitement. "Thanks, Pine. I'll do just what you said!" She turned to Sendi. "Do you mind looking for your cat alone for a while? I must get on with my major mission!"

Sendi knew it wouldn't do any good to beg Gwen to put aside her major mission, even for a while. "I can look for my cat alone, Gwen. I'll see you later." Sendi looked up at Pine.

"Bye for now. I'll be back later to see if the cat came back."

"You might want to name that old stray cat. A name's mighty important, you know," said Pine.

Sendi nodded thoughtfully. "I'll think of a name," she said.

She ran to her house and checked the bushes there while she muttered, "Tom. Kitty. Scruffy. Half Ear. Stripe. Blacky." She rubbed sweat off her face, leaving behind a streak of dirt. None of the names were right for the huge striped stray cat.

Watching carefully for the cat, she walked down the sidewalk toward the corner store where she'd seen him this morning. She saw Diane playing with two girls on the porch of a green house, but she kept walking, holding her breath in case Diane spotted her. She didn't want Diane to know anything about the cat or her great plans to cage him. Diane would scare the cat away on purpose or even set him free from the cage.

Just then Sendi thought of old man Monroe. Momma cleaned house for him, and sometimes she had taken Sendi with her so Sendi wouldn't have to be home alone. The stray cat reminded Sendi of Monroe. He didn't want anyone to touch him, and he didn't trust anyone, not even Momma who had cleaned his house since Grandpa had divorced her. Suddenly Sendi missed Momma and the talks they'd had. She missed her old bike that Mom had bought at a yard sale for five dollars. Mom had left it behind when they'd moved away from Momma's house because there wasn't room to carry it. Sendi sighed as she stepped over a crack in the sidewalk. She even missed Monroe and his shaky voice.

"Monroe," whispered Sendi. "That's what I'll name my cat." She smiled. "Monroe."

Sendi walked around a toy truck in the middle of the sidewalk.

"Monroe," she whispered again. When Monroe learned to trust her and love her, she'd write a letter to Momma and tell her all about him.

But would Mom let her keep the cat when they didn't even have enough money for groceries this week?

Sendi pushed the terrible thought aside. She'd somehow talk Mom into letting her keep the cat. Maybe she could find a way to make enough money to buy cat food every week herself.

"I wish we'd stayed with Momma," muttered Sendi. Then she shook her head. It was hard living on their own, but Mom said it was important.

"I'm twenty-two years old, Sendi," Mom had said. "I can't live with Momma all my life and let her take care of us. It's time I started acting like an adult. I want a home of my own, and I want to make my own way. Someday I want a husband to love me."

Sendi waited for a car; then she crossed the street. If Mom did get married, it would be strange to have a man live with them. Maybe Mom could marry Pine. He was nice. But maybe Mom would think he was too old. He was almost as old as old man Monroe.

Just then Sendi caught sight of the stray cat. "Monroe," she said. Her heart leaped. Thoughts of everything but Monroe left her mind. He was walking in the area where she'd seen him this morning before Diane had started chasing her.

"Your name is Monroe," she whispered as she crept toward him. Monroe walked across a backyard one house away from the corner store. The house was big and needed paint. The grass hadn't been cut in a long time, and garbage was piled high around a rusty barrel.

Sendi stopped just at the edge of the yard. If she walked toward Monroe, would he turn and run? Would the person who lived in the house chase Monroe away?

Sendi locked her suddenly icy hands behind her back and stood very still.

5

Sendi's Secret

Sendi stepped forward two steps, and then stopped to watch Monroe. A blue jay scolded from the top of a maple tree. Loud music blared from a car driving past.

Suddenly the back door of the house opened a crack. Sendi's heart dropped to her feet. What if the person wanted to kill Monroe? Sendi wanted to grab him and carry him to safety. But she couldn't move and couldn't yell out a warning.

As she watched, Monroe walked toward the open door, his long tail high, the tip swishing back and forth. A shiver ran down Sendi's spine, but still she couldn't move and couldn't speak.

The door opened wider, and an old woman with ratty gray hair and a faded cotton dress covered with a tattered apron stepped halfway out. "Kitty," she said softly.

A cry rose up in Sendi's throat, but couldn't get past the dry lump. She wanted to leap the space between her and Monroe, catch him, and run to her house with him where she'd love him and feed him and keep him safe.

"Kitty," the woman said softly again.

Monroe sped across the grass and leaped right up into the woman's arms. She laughed and hugged the huge cat close. Monroe licked her face all over. She giggled and then slipped inside and closed the door.

Sendi stared at the closed door for a long time. Finally she sank weakly to the ground, hot tears burning her eyes. Monroe wasn't a stray after all! He belonged to the old woman in the old house! He had leaped into her arms, and he had kissed her all over her face. He belonged to her! Oh, it was too awful to think about!

"He's not a stray," Sendi whispered hoarsely. The cat she loved and wanted belonged to someone else. She knuckled away her tears and slowly stood and stared at the back door of the run-down house for a long time. Finally she walked down the sidewalk toward home. Her eyes filled with tears. Unable to see where she was going, she bumped right into a teenage boy with a black ponytail. He wore black designer jeans and a white tee shirt with words across the front.

"Hey, kid, watch where you're going," he said gruffly as he pushed her aside.

Sendi mumbled, "Sorry." She wiped away her tears and sniffed hard. It would be terrible if anyone else saw her cry.

At her house she crept inside and

sprawled across her bed, her arm over her eyes. Her head buzzed with thoughts of Monroe. The terrible picture of Monroe leaping into the old woman's arms and kissing her face played over and over in her head.

After a long time, she splashed cold water on her face, rubbed it dry, and walked outdoors. The hot sun burned against her. The only sound she heard was the hum of the air conditioner at Gwen's house.

Sendi bit her bottom lip. She had to tell Pine to forget about baiting the trap. He could put the cage back in his garage where he'd found it.

She walked across her yard and glanced toward the big tree where the Roscommons had their treehouse. She saw a flash of red. Then Diane peeked out the door.

"Sendi, want to come up and play?" asked Diane.

Sendi stopped short. Diane usually wanted the treehouse to herself when it was her turn to play in it. "Why do you want me to come play?" Sendi asked with a suspicious frown.

"I just do," said Diane.

Sendi knew she should go tell Pine about Monroe, but she walked to the base of the tree and looked up the ladder. "You won't step on my hands, will you, Diane?"

"No!" Diane shook her head. "I'm going to be nice. I promise."

Sendi hesitated. Then she climbed the tree and stood inside the treehouse with Diane. "How come you're going to be nice?"

Diane shrugged. "I just am. I got cookies. Want one?"

"Sure." Sendi sat cross-legged in the middle of the floor with Diane in front of her, their knees almost touching.

Diane took a bite of a cookie, and then said, "I wonder if we'll be in the same room next week when school starts."

"How many fourth grades are there?" asked Sendi.

"Four." Diane wolfed two cookies down. "Donny had Miss Taylor last year, and he said she gives too much homework. I sure don't want Miss Taylor."

"I don't like homework much," said Sendi.

Diane leaned forward. "Now that I'm so nice, will you tell me why you ran away from me this morning?"

Sendi sighed loud and long. She might as well tell since Monroe belonged to someone already. "I was trying to find the striped stray cat."

"Why?" asked Diane.

"I just wanted to," said Sendi. "I thought if you saw him, you'd chase him away."

"I would've. I hate cats. Even Camille," Diane said as she reached for another cookie.

"Do you like dogs?" asked Sendi.

Diane shrugged. "I guess. But not cats. They eat birds. It would be terrible if the cats ate all the birds."

"Camille doesn't eat birds," said Sendi. "Gwen feeds her cat food."

Diane flipped back her dark hair. "I

saw Camille eat a bird. Actually eat a bird! I almost threw up!"

"I saw Monroe eat a moth. I almost threw up," said Sendi.

"Who's Monroe?" asked Diane with a frown.

Sendi's shoulders drooped. "The old stray cat I was talking about."

"How can a stray cat have a name?" asked Diane.

"I named him," said Sendi. She started to tell Diane about the old woman, but just then Diane's mom called her. Diane scrambled down the tree, taking her cookies with her.

Sendi slowly climbed down and walked to Pine's house. She might as well tell him the bad news.

As she approached, Pine came around the side of his house. "Sendi, good news," he said, smiling.

"What?" she asked with a long face.

"Come and look!" Pine motioned for her to follow him, and he walked to the cage. "Look! We caught the old stray."

Sendi stared down at Monroe in the cage. Pine had already hooked the collar in place. Light flashed off the diamond-like studs as Monroe moved his head, trying to knock off the collar. "You caught him!" whispered Sendi as shivers ran up and down her spine.

"Sure did," said Pine proudly. He rubbed a leathery old hand over his leathery old face. "And not a hair on him was hurt."

"You caught Monroe," said Sendi as she sank to her knees beside the cage.

Pine hunkered down beside her and looked at the cat too. "So you gave him a name?"

"Yes. Monroe," said Sendi around the hard lump in her throat.

"Monroe." Pine chuckled. "Monroe it is."

"Can I touch him?" asked Sendi.

"Not yet." Pine lifted his hat, scratched his head, and settled his hat back in place. "He's mighty upset that he's locked up, and he don't care much for that collar. But he's not as wild as I thought, so you feed him a couple of days, and he'll let you pet him before you know it."

Slowly Sendi stood. She had to tell Pine that Monroe wasn't really a stray and that he must set him free, but she couldn't do it. She wanted Monroe for herself. That old woman probably had other pets and lots of friends. She didn't need Monroe.

Sendi laced her icy fingers together. She needed Monroe worse than anyone had ever needed a pet.

Monroe yowled and tried to scratch his way out.

"I hate to see him locked up," said Pine as he stood. "But it's better for him. If he was running loose, somebody could run over him with a car, or the city could catch him and take him to the pound and destroy him. Yes, it's a lot better for him to be here for a while until he's used to you and his collar."

Sendi nodded. She would teach him to love her, and she'd love him more than anyone else ever had! "I'll take good care of him, Pine. I promise."

"I'm sure you will." Pine patted Sendi's shoulder. Sendi stepped closer to Pine and watched Monroe twist back and forth in the cage to try to find a way out. She pushed her terrible secret deep inside herself and locked the door on it. No one would ever know that Monroe belonged to the old woman.

A dark cloud settled over Sendi, and she couldn't find a smile even when Pine said he'd help teach Monroe tricks once he was out of the cage.

Sendi sank to the grass beside the cage. She sat with her elbows on her knees and her chin in her hands as she watched Monroe. She had a cat, a cat of her very own. But she couldn't smile even a tiny smile.

6

Plans

Sendi stepped inside the kitchen to find Mom already home. Her perfume and the smell that she carried home from the salon hung in the air. She'd changed from her pink uniform to her tan shorts and an orange oversized blouse. Orange and yellow earrings dangled from her ears to her plump shoulders.

"Hi, Sendi," Janice said. "I was ready to go out looking for you."

"Why?" asked Sendi as she sat at the table and leaned her head on her crossed arms.

"Momma called me at work this afternoon," said Janice as she dropped the dishtowel and sat at the tiny table across from Sendi. Janice looked ready to cry. "She's coming to see us."

Sendi's face lit up, and then fell. Momma could see right through her. She'd know there was some hidden secret locked away inside her, and she wouldn't quit asking until Sendi told her everything. "When is she coming?"

"Thursday. Day after tomorrow." Janice's hand shook as she tucked a strand of blonde hair back in her french braid. "I don't know if I can handle having her come."

"Me neither," said Sendi with a long sigh.

"She'll want to know how much money I got in the bank and if we have enough to eat." Janice shook her head, sending her earrings dancing. "I don't want her to know I'm short of money and that you take care of yourself all day long. She'd make me go back home."

"But this is home now," said Sendi. "You said so." She couldn't go back to live with Momma or she'd have to give up Monroe.

Janice nodded, and then nodded harder. "That's right! I am twenty-two years old, and I am an adult. I don't need my mother telling me what I can and can't do!" She sagged in her chair. "Oh, but I wish I'd told her to wait and come next month when I have things more together."

"You could call her back and tell her," said Sendi.

"Then she'd know for sure something was wrong." Janice walked to the refrigerator and jerked it open. It was almost bare. Cool air flowed out with the smell of cantaloupe.

"How hungry are you, Sendi? How about a slice of cantaloupe and a bowl of cornflakes?"

"I'm not very hungry," said Sendi.

"Did you eat all the ice cream bars again?"

"No." Sendi shook her head. She'd done that once and been spanked for it.

"Then what's wrong?" asked Janice with a scowl.

"Nothing." Sendi twisted the tail of her tee shirt around her finger. "Did you ask Momma to bring my bike?"

"No, but she said she'd bring it."

"Great!" But Sendi couldn't feel good even about having her bike.

"I told her it was too old and too much bother, but she said she knew you loved that old thing, so she's bringing it." Janice sliced up cantaloupe into a bowl, handed it to Sendi to set on the table, and plopped the box of cornflakes on the counter along with two spoons and two bowls. "Get the sugar, Sendi."

Several minutes later, Sendi dried the few dishes as Janice washed them and handed them to her.

"You're awful quiet tonight," said Janice. "You sure nothing's wrong?"

Sendi shook her head. She desperately wanted to tell Mom everything, but she just couldn't.

"I know what'll make you happy," said Janice.

"What?" Sendi hung up the dishtowel and turned to Janice.

"Today I got a frame for only a quarter, and we're going to frame your birth certificate and hang it on your wall."

Sendi's eyes lit up. "Thanks, Mom!"

"Now you won't have to tuck it away in your coloring book, but you can have it where you can see it all the time." Janice laughed softly. "I been trying my best to act like a mom should act. A mom should do things for her kid, you know."

Sendi flushed and looked down at her feet.

"Run and get the certificate, and let's get it hung." Janice laid the frame on the table while Sendi ran to her bedroom.

A little later Janice hung the certificate near the light switch in Sendi's room. "It's eye level for you so you can read it any time you want," she said.

Sendi looked at it for a long time, but she'd already memorized everything on it. She knew for sure she wasn't an alien like kids said. She did have a mom. She had a dad too, but his name wasn't on the birth certificate.

"I did something else today, too," said Janice with a catch in her voice.

Sendi looked up at her questioningly.

"I asked Momma to get your dad's address." Janice took a deep breath, and Sendi stood frozen in place. "I'm going to write to him and tell him all about you, even if he doesn't want to know. I'll send him a picture of you so he can see what a pretty girl you are."

Sendi shivered. "He probably will think I'm ugly," she whispered hoarsely.

"He might be too angry to look at the picture, but I'll send it anyway." Janice slipped her arm around Sendi's shoulder. "I want to be a good mom to you, but I still got a lot to learn."

Sendi flung her arms around Janice and hugged her tight. Then she jumped back, her face flaming. They didn't hug and kiss in her family, and Mom might be mad.

Janice flicked away a tear. "You go out and play a while if you want. I want to watch TV and have some time alone. But you be in before dark!"

Sendi nodded, looked at her framed birth certificate one more time, and ran out the back door. The sun was bright, but had lost a lot of its heat. She still felt all warm inside from hugging Mom. Maybe someday she could hug her any time she wanted and sit on her lap even though she was a big girl of nine.

She smiled, and then thought of Monroe. The smile vanished. She ran to Pine's house and knocked on his back door.

When he opened it, she heard his TV in the background. For once he wasn't wearing his big cowboy hat. Wisps of gray hair stuck up on his almost bald head. "Howdy, Sendi," he said.

"I came to feed Monroe," she said in a small voice.

"Go right ahead," he said.

Sendi swallowed hard. "I . . . I don't have anything to feed him."

"I got a hotdog you can give him." Pine disappeared inside and stepped out a minute later with a hotdog in his hand and his hat on his head. He handed the hotdog to Sendi as they walked to the cage. "I already gave Monroe water. Poor cat sure hates being in that cage."

Guilt rose inside Sendi, and she almost blurted out the truth. But when she saw Monroe, the words died in her throat. She wanted Monroe more than she'd ever wanted anything. Well, almost anything. She wanted a dad of her own even more than she wanted a cat.

She knelt down beside the cage. "Here, Monroe. Here's a nice hotdog for you. It's good. You'll like it a lot." She held the hotdog out, and Monroe sniffed it.

"He won't eat it while you're holding it," said Pine.

She pushed it through the wire and let it drop near Monroe's foot. "You go ahead and eat it, Monroe. I know you're hungry."

Monroe batted it with his paw, and then bit into it, tearing a piece off.

Just then Gwen ran into the yard. "Hi, Sendi. Hi, Pine. Oh, I see your cat is eating."

"I named him Monroe," said Sendi.

Gwen sank to the ground beside Sendi and Pine. "Monroe," Gwen said as if trying it out to see if she liked it. "You sure can't feed him hotdogs all the time. Will you buy him cat food like I do for Camille?"

"I guess," said Sendi. But where would she get the money? She'd have to think of something.

Pine stood up, and his bones cracked sharply. "Old bones," he said with a chuckle. "I'm going back inside. You girls stay as long as you want, but don't try to touch Monroe. He's still pretty mad about being locked up."

"We won't touch him," said Gwen.

A band squeezed Sendi's heart. Oh, she should ask Pine to take off the collar and let Monroe go free! But she kept her mouth closed tight.

"See you tomorrow, girls," said Pine.

"Are we still going to the park?" asked Gwen.

"Sure," said Pine.

Gwen turned to Sendi. "Pine said we could meet his grandkids in the park tomorrow afternoon. He's baby-sitting them there. Want to go with us?"

Sendi hesitated, and then nodded. Maybe if she kept really busy, she wouldn't have time to think about how wrong she was to keep Monroe from going home where he really belonged.

Sendi watched Monroe tear off another piece of hotdog. A tear welled up in her eye, spilled over, and slipped down her pale cheek.

7

The Job

Sendi gripped the bed sheet and strained to hear Mom close the door, start her car, and drive away. She forced herself to stay in bed another whole minute. Then she leaped up and dressed in clean blue shorts and her tee shirt with the rainbow on it.

She ran out the back door without taking time for even a slice of toast. All the way to the corner store she ran, and then stopped at the door and took a deep breath. A pleasantly cool wind blew against her. Cars drove past on the busy street next to the store. She glanced around, but didn't see anyone she knew. Today she surely didn't want Diane to see her here.

Slowly she pushed open the door. A bell tinkled over it, and Mrs. Wells behind the counter looked up and smiled. She was tall and thin with dark hair and black eyes.

"Good morning," Mrs. Wells said as she smoothed her gray shirt down over her gray slacks. "Can I help you find something?"

Sendi walked to the counter and looked up. She took a deep breath. Last night she'd decided what to do. But it was easier to do in her imagination than in real life. "I'm Sendi Mason, and I live a couple of blocks away."

"Yes?" The woman lifted a dark brow. "Oh, I remember seeing you in here with Gwen."

"That's right," said Sendi, feeling a little better.

"What can I do for you?" asked Mrs. Wells as she tucked a strand of dark hair behind her ear.

"I need to buy a can of cat food for my cat, but I don't have any money." Sweat popped out on Sendi's forehead. But she gathered her courage. "If you'll let me take a can of cat food, I'll work for it. I can sweep the floor or dust off the cans. But I don't know how to run the cash register."

Mrs. Wells smiled. "Well, Sendi, I just might have something you can do." She walked around the counter, leaned against it, and crossed her thin arms. "I just might have."

Sendi's heart leaped. "I'll do anything!"

Mrs. Wells laughed. "*Anything* covers a lot of territory." She narrowed her black eyes thoughtfully. "Mrs. Yeetter called about ten minutes ago to ask if I could bring a few things to her. I said I would, but I haven't been able to get away. You take the bag of groceries to her, and I'll give you two cans of cat food. Want the job?"

Sendi's eyes flashed with excitement. "Yes! But where does Mrs. Yeetter live?"

"Here's her address, and here's the bag. Just walk out the door, and it's the big old house with the wide front porch. The house numbers are next to her door. You have to use the front door, or she won't answer. She says her back door sticks." Mrs. Wells smiled and patted Sendi's arm. "Come right back after you deliver the groceries, and I'll have the cat food waiting."

"Oh, thank you!" Sendi gripped the bag tightly as she walked out the door. She giggled. This was her first real job! She'd do it well just in case Mrs. Wells needed her to do it again.

Sendi walked down the sidewalk of the busy street. She'd never walked on that sidewalk before. Cars whizzed past. One honked and brakes squealed.

Sendi found the house with the wide front porch and the big numbers next to the door. She trembled. It looked like a haunted house. The front yard was small, and the grass needed to be cut. A bush with tiny green leaves partly covered a corner of the porch.

Slowly she walked up the wide steps. A shiver ran down her spine. She knocked on the door with the heavy brass knocker. Her heart beat as loudly as the knocker. She waited, listening for any sound from inside. The street sounds covered all other sounds.

Was Mrs. Yeetter home?

Sendi shifted the bag in her arms and knocked again. Her mouth suddenly felt bone dry.

Slowly the door opened a crack. "What d' you want?" The woman's voice cracked just like a witch's voice on TV. Sendi wanted to turn and run.

"Mrs. Wells asked me to deliver your groceries, Mrs. Yeetter," said Sendi, shivering.

"How do I know you're not out to kill me?"

"You're Mrs. Yeetter, aren't you?"

"Yes."

Sendi licked her dry lips. "Mrs. Wells said to bring the groceries to you. I can set them down right here and leave. Then you can get them if you want."

"No!" Mrs. Yeetter opened the door wider, and Sendi almost dropped the bag of groceries.

Mrs. Yeetter was Monroe's owner! She wore the same clothes that she'd worn yesterday. Her hair was just as tangled and matted.

Sendi couldn't believe her eyes. This was the house that Monroe lived in! Sendi had never seen the front of the big house before and didn't realize the backyard was big enough to come out to the other street.

"I can't carry that whole heavy bag," said Mrs. Yeetter. "You carry it to the kitchen, but don't you dare steal anything. I mean it! I got eyes like a hawk!" Mrs. Yeetter opened the door wide enough for Sendi to enter.

Sendi trembled. Oh, she didn't want to be here!

"Follow me," said Mrs. Yeetter. She shuffled along a dim hallway stacked with newspapers and boxes and stopped in the messy kitchen. "Set the bag right there on the table."

There was only one clear spot on the table, and Sendi carefully set the bag down.

"That cat of mine," muttered Mrs. Yeetter, shaking her head.

"Cat?" asked Sendi hoarsely.

"My old tomcat didn't come home last night. And he knows I worry about him." Mrs. Yeetter fingered the pocket on her faded apron. "I told him I wouldn't put up with him staying out all night."

Sendi moved from one foot to the other. How she wanted to run away!

"I had him since he was a tiny scrap of fur," she said gruffly.

Sendi bit her bottom lip.

"He almost died, but I fed him with a little bottle, and I kept him alive." Mrs. Yeetter flicked a tear off her stubby eyelash.

Tears burned the backs of Sendi's eyes.

"What's your name?" snapped Mrs. Yeetter.

Sendi swallowed hard. "Sendi Mason."

"Don't think I'm paying you for this," said Mrs. Yeetter sharply.

"I know you're not," said Sendi.

"Well, you know more than I do!" Mrs. Yeetter reached for an old purse that hung on the back of a kitchen chair.

"You don't have to pay me," said Sendi. "I don't want you to." She couldn't take money from the woman she'd stolen Monroe from! Oh, she had to get away before she blurted out the truth about Monroe.

"Well, I'm going to!" Mrs. Yeetter rummaged in her purse and finally pulled out a coin. "Don't think you're going to get rich off me, little girl, because you aren't! Now, take this!"

Sendi reluctantly reached for the coin and saw that it was a dime. She held it as if it burned her fingers.

"What d' you say?" asked Mrs. Yeetter in her sharp voice.

"Thank you," mumbled Sendi.

"You're welcome. Now get out of here, and don't steal anything as you go!"

Sendi walked as fast as she dared down the dim hall to the front door. She stepped out on the porch, took a deep steadying breath, and ran back to the corner store.

Mrs. Wells had the cans of cat food in a small bag. She held it out to Sendi. "Here you are, Sendi. Thank you very much."

"You're welcome."

"Did she scare you?" asked Mrs. Wells with a grin.

"A little, I guess," said Sendi.

"She's harmless. She's a lonely old lady with only her cat to keep her company." Mrs. Wells sighed and shook her head.

Sendi's stomach knotted painfully. "I'd better go," she whispered.

"See you again, Sendi," said Mrs. Wells, smiling.

Sendi nodded and went outdoors. She walked slowly away from the store and stopped on the sidewalk at Mrs. Yeetter's big backyard. In her mind she saw the door open and Monroe leap into Mrs. Yeetter's arms and kiss her all over her face.

With a moan Sendi dashed away and didn't stop running until she reached Pine's house.

He was already outdoors talking to Monroe. "Morning, Sendi," Pine said, pushing his hat back.

"I brought cat food," said Sendi breathlessly. "And I brought a dime to pay for the hotdog." She held out the bag and the dime.

Pine grinned, slipped the dime in his Levis pocket, and lifted a can of cat food out of the bag. "I'll get a can opener, and we'll feed our friend together. He's settled down some this morning."

Sendi wanted to run home and never see Monroe again, but she walked to the cage and looked down at him. He seemed tired and unhappy. He turned his head and gazed right at her. She almost burst into tears.

Behind her Pine came with an open can of cat food. The smell drifted out, and Sendi wrinkled her nose.

"Do you want to give it to him?" asked Pine, holding the can out to her.

She shook her head. "You go ahead."

"He won't hurt you," said Pine. "I even had him out of the cage on a leash, and he didn't try to hurt me. But he did act like he wanted free."

Sendi's stomach knotted, but she didn't say anything as she watched Pine feed Monroe. Monroe ate the food as if he enjoyed it, but even that didn't make her feel better.

"What's wrong, Sendi?" asked Pine softly.

She shrugged.

"I know it's hard to see the big stray cat caged like this, but you can take him out on the leash until he learns that he belongs to you." Pine hunkered down beside Sendi. She smelled the leather of his boots and felt the warmth of his arm, but she couldn't look at him for fear of bursting into tears. "He's a smart fella. He should be out of that cage by next week."

Sendi thought of lonely Mrs. Yeetter. What would she do if she never saw her cat again?

Pine cleared his throat. "Are you having second thoughts about keeping Monroe?"

"No!" cried Sendi, shaking her head hard.

"He's a big responsibility, and it will take extra money to feed him," said Pine. "I'd understand if you wanted me to open the cage and set him free."

Sendi trembled. Then she jumped up. She knotted her fists at her sides and jutted out her chin. "Monroe is my cat, and I want to keep him forever!"

She spun on her heels and ran home.

8

Momma's Visit

Sendi ran to the car as Momma climbed out. Momma was plump like Mom, and she had her short curly hair dyed light brown. She wore tan shorts and a big brown and tan shirt with splashes of orange. Orange earrings dangled from her ears.

"Sendi!" Momma cried. To Sendi's surprise she caught her close and held her so tight Sendi couldn't breathe. But it was a good feeling. Suddenly Momma let her go, stepped back, and looked at her. "I see you got your hair brushed, and you're wearing clean clothes. Did you clean your room and make your bed this morning?"

"Yes, Momma." Sendi peeked around the back of Momma's car to see her old blue bike tied in place on the trunk. "You brought it! Thank you, Momma!"

Momma looked pleased, but only shrugged. "You need a bike. How will you get those leg muscles developed if you don't have a bike?" She worked on the rope and finally got the knots loose. She lifted the bike down and rolled it to Sendi, and then pulled off the blanket that had protected the trunk.

Sendi stroked the bike's rusty handlebars and patted the torn padding on the seat. Her bike! She rode around in a tight circle, and then leaned the bike against the tree beside the driveway. "I'm glad you brought it, Momma."

Momma nodded and smiled. "Me, too."

She unlocked the trunk and tossed the blanket inside. "I brought some other things too."

"You did?" Sendi peered inside the wide trunk and saw several brown paper bags. Mom would be mad when she saw the food, but Sendi was glad, especially when she saw the big bag of oranges.

"Groceries," said Momma. "I know how hard it is to get started on your own. Janice didn't say a word about being short of things, but I read between the lines." Momma always talked like that, but Sendi knew what she meant. Sendi lifted out a bag that held boxes of cereal and a bag of sugar.

"When will Janice get home?" asked Momma as she lifted out two bags and carried them toward the door.

"She said she'd try to be here around 1 if she could get off," said Sendi as she eased open the screen door and held it wide for Momma.

"It's almost 1 now. That means you and me better get some fast talking in.

Once your mom gets here we won't have a chance." Momma set the bags on the table and hurried out to get the others. "We'll talk while we put these away."

Sendi's stomach knotted. She didn't want Momma to look into her heart and see the terrible secret she had locked inside. She slid a gallon of milk into the refrigerator and hid her burning face from Momma. "Did you get any more cleaning jobs since we left, Momma?"

"One. From an old woman who has trouble seeing." Momma turned away from the cupboard and shook her head, sending her earrings dancing. "You never saw so much dust in all your life. I thought I'd have to wear an oxygen mask." She rubbed her nose as if she were going to sneeze just thinking about it. "But I got it cleaned, and it won't take much to keep it clean." She stuck a bottle of dish soap under the sink. "She has a cat."

Sendi stiffened and almost dropped the bag of noodles. Momma chuckled. "It's some cat. Pearl's her name. She's gray and has hair that Janice could curl. She can ring the doorbell with her paw."

"How?" asked Sendi even though she hadn't wanted to. Talking about a cat was too dangerous.

"Mrs. Perkins set a stepladder near the back door and when Pearl wants in, she climbs the ladder and rings the doorbell." Momma laughed. "Funniest thing you ever saw."

Sendi didn't want to talk about Pearl or any cat. "What about old man Monroe? How's he doing?"

"Fine for a man his age. He talks more to me than he used to. I guess he knows he can trust me." Momma dropped four cans of frozen orange juice in the freezer section of the refrigerator. "But I want to hear about you, Sendi. What do you do all day long?"

Sendi shrugged. She felt a flush creeping up her neck and over her face. "I play with my friends. We go to the park." She had gone to the park with Pine and Gwen Wednesday, but she hadn't stayed long.

She'd met Pine's grandkids, but hadn't talked to them much. Yesterday she'd stayed in the house watching TV most of the day. "But now I have my bike to ride," she said.

Just then the door opened, and Janice rushed in. "Momma!" To Sendi's surprise they hugged and then stood apart and just looked at each other. Finally Janice noticed the pile of folded paper bags on the table.

"Momma! You brought groceries! You know you didn't need to do that," said Janice, blinking back tears. "I'm a big girl now, Momma. I don't need you taking care of me."

Momma shrugged. "So, I can bring you a gift if I want, can't I? I'm still your momma no matter how old you are."

"I know," said Janice in a tiny voice. "But I want to learn to stand on my own two feet."

"So learn with food in your cupboards," said Momma as she grabbed up the empty bags and stacked them under the sink in a neat pile. "Did you have lunch yet?"

Janice laughed and shook her head. "But you sit down and let me fix lunch for you." She turned to Sendi. "Did you already eat?"

Sendi nodded. She'd had a hard time forcing any food down, but she'd eaten half a bologna sandwich and an ice cream bar.

"Run out and play then while Momma and I talk," said Janice. "I'll change my clothes and see what food Momma brought."

Sendi walked outdoors to her bike and just stood beside it. She was glad Momma had brought it, but for some reason she didn't feel glad. She felt dirty inside.

Just then Diane came up. "Is that your bike?" asked Diane as she touched the front tire.

Sendi nodded. "And don't you dare make fun of it!"

Diane's eyes widened. "I wouldn't do that! I like it. It looks like it would be fun to ride." She sighed loud and long. "I don't even have a bike. I had a trike when I was little. My brothers have bikes, but they won't let me even touch them."

"You can ride my bike if you want," said Sendi. She thought being nice to Diane would take away the terrible ache inside her, but it didn't. Maybe the ache would be there forever.

Diane pedaled the bike around the yard, wobbling as if she'd fall over any second. "This is great!" she cried. "Look how good I'm doing!"

Sendi sat on the grass and leaned against the tree while she watched Diane having fun. Sendi brushed the grass that tickled her legs. Everybody in the whole world except her was having fun.

Camille ambled into the yard, walked right up to Sendi, and curled up on her lap, purring so loudly that Sendi thought people for miles around could hear.

Sendi stared down at Camille, and then gingerly stroked her long white neck. She touched Camille's collar, but jerked her hand away. Abruptly she pushed

Camille off her lap. "Get away from me,"
she snapped.

Camille rubbed against Sendi's legs,
and then walked off to her own yard.

Sendi closed her eyes and groaned.

"What's wrong?" asked Diane as she
straddled the bike just a few inches from
Sendi.

Sendi bit her bottom lip.

"You don't want to tell me, do you?"
Diane flipped back her hair. "You think I
can't keep a secret, don't you?"

"I didn't say that," said Sendi.

Diane leaned down until her head was
close to Sendi's. "I know a secret."

Sendi frowned. "So?"

"I know that Monroe really belongs to
old Mrs. Yeetter who lives near the corner
store," said Diane.

Sendi gasped and leaped to her feet,
her cheeks flushed bright red. "How do you
know that?"

Diane shrugged. "I always knew it."
Diane looked around to make sure no one
was listening, and then whispered,

"Sometimes I visit Mrs. Yeetter. I let her tell me all the old stories about when she was a girl my age. I get bored, but I never tell her. I feel sorry for her because she's all alone. And she's so ragged and dirty."

Sendi stared in surprise at Diane. "Why didn't you tell her that I have Monroe?" asked Sendi gruffly.

Diane brushed an ant off her foot. "I knew you loved Monroe and wanted him for your own pet."

"But Mrs. Yeetter loves Monroe!" cried Sendi.

"I know," said Diane, looking sad.

"And he loves her," whispered Sendi.

"I know," said Diane.

Sendi covered her face with trembling hands.

"You could give the cat back," said Diane softly.

Sendi dropped her knotted fists to her sides and glared at Diane. "No way! And don't you dare tell!"

"I won't." Diane narrowed her eyes. "As

long as you let me ride your bike anytime I want," she said.

"Ride it forever!" snapped Sendi. "See if I care!" Diane rode away just as Gwen ran up to Sendi.

"Guess what?" cried Gwen, dancing from one foot to the other.

"What?" asked Sendi, even though she wanted Gwen to leave her alone in her misery.

Gwen's eyes sparkled with excitement. "Mom and Dad just took me to the library so I could read information on drugs to help me with my major mission! They said lots of kids our age don't know what drugs look like, and so if somebody offered us some, we wouldn't even know it was drugs." Gwen leaned closer to Sendi and dropped her voice almost to a whisper. "Even I didn't know what some of the drugs looked like."

Sendi didn't know either, but she didn't say so.

"Now when I warn kids about drugs, I

can tell them what they look like, and it'll help them know more to say no to drugs!" Gwen laughed and spun around. "This is a wonderful mission, Sendi! Want to come home with me and look at some pictures of drugs that I brought home?"

Sendi shook her head. "My grandma's here, and I want to visit with her." The lie seemed to burn through her tongue. Momma was indeed visiting, but Sendi knew she was to stay outdoors until they called her in. They had a lot to talk about, and they didn't want Sendi to listen.

"How long is she staying?" asked Gwen.

"Until in the morning," said Sendi. She knew she'd sleep on the couch tonight so Momma could have her bed. But she didn't mind at all.

Gwen looked more closely at Sendi. "Something's wrong with you, Sendi."

Sendi locked her fingers together. If she wasn't careful, she'd burst into tears and tell Gwen everything.

"What is wrong?" asked Gwen softly. Sendi shook her head.

"Do you want to come home and talk to my mom and dad? They'll help you. They always help me," said Gwen.

Tears burned Sendi's eyes, but she blinked them away. "I don't need any help, Gwen. Go do your great mission, and leave me alone!

Gwen's lip trembled as she turned and walked slowly away. Sendi rubbed her nose with the back of her hand and sank back to the ground under the tree.

9

The Park

Sendi stood beside Janice and waved as Momma drove away. Janice sighed, and Sendi blinked away tears. A robin landed on a branch and sang.

"It wasn't so bad after all," said Janice as she tugged her pink uniform back in place. "She didn't scold me or anything."

Sendi nodded. "She didn't scold me either."

Janice turned Sendi to her and looked closely at her. "I'd sure like to know what's wrong with you. You've been walking around as if you're going to cry if I even look at you."

"I'm okay, Mom," whispered Sendi. She didn't want Mom to ask again, or she just might break down and tell her. But it did feel good to have Mom notice. She never had before.

"You didn't even ask me about . . . about that address," said Janice, her face brick red and her eyes sparkling with unshed tears.

"What address?" asked Sendi with a slight frown.

"I knew it!" cried Janice. "Something is wrong! I don't have time to make you tell me now, but when I get home from work, we'll have a talk. One of those talks that you and Momma used to have."

Sendi cringed. What would she do now? But maybe Mom would be too tired after work to talk. She usually was.

"You be good today, Sendi," said

Janice as she opened her car door. "And don't watch TV all day long. I mean it!"

"I won't," said Sendi.

She watched Janice drive away, the warm sun reflecting off the car. Then she walked slowly down the sidewalk to Pine's house. She couldn't stay away any longer.

Pine was feeding and watering Monroe. He rubbed his jaw and looked down at Sendi with a frown. "I was beginning to get worried about you, Sendi girl."

"I . . . I just couldn't come sooner," she said. She peeked around at Monroe. "He looks happy," she whispered.

"He's glad to be fed regular," said Pine. "But he'll be glad to get out of that cage. I was just ready to take him out on a leash. Now that you're here, you can do it."

Her hand trembled as she held the leash that Pine snapped to Monroe's collar. Pine's green plaid shirt looked bright next to Monroe's dark hair.

Monroe meowed and walked out. He rubbed against Pine's boot, and then against Sendi's ankle. Her breath caught in her throat, and she smiled.

"He likes me!" she said in awe.

"It won't be long before you can turn him loose, and he'll stay right with you," said Pine as he pushed his hat back.

Carefully she touched Monroe. He didn't jump away or try to scratch her, so she petted his back and between his ears. He felt soft and smelled like fish.

"You got yourself a fine pet," said Pine, standing with his thumbs looped in his belt. "It should make you real happy."

Sendi waited for happiness to spread inside her and bubble up through her, but nothing happened. She held the leash out to Pine. "I have to get home. I'll bring food later for Monroe." She'd get the can of tuna that Momma had brought.

Pine caught Sendi's arm, and she stopped, but couldn't look at him.

"Sendi girl, if something's troubling you, you can tell me, and I'll help," he said.

"I'm all right," she said around the lump in her throat.

"I can't stand to see that long face," he said. "You can trust me, you know."

"I know," she whispered. Slowly she walked away from Pine and away from Monroe.

Later she leaned against the inside of her kitchen door and took a deep, steadying breath. After leaving Pine she'd jumped rope a hundred times without missing, watched the Hansen boys wrestle, tried to do handstands, and rode her bike around the block before Diane wanted it again. She wanted to keep her mind off the terrible secret. Still thoughts of Monroe and Mrs. Yeetter burned in her brain. "I will not let myself feel so bad that I turn Monroe loose. I will forget all about Mrs. Yeetter!"

Oh, but that would be hard! "I'll do it anyway," she whispered.

Just then someone knocked, and Sendi jumped almost out of her skin. She opened the door to find Gwen standing there, smiling and happy as if everything were wonderful everywhere. Sendi almost slammed the door in her face.

"Hi, Sendi," said Gwen, walking right in. She wore bright red shorts and a pink tee shirt with big red, yellow, and white balloons all over the front of it. "Pine says he's going to the park. Want to go?"

Sendi thought about it and then decided it would be better than staying by herself. "I got to get the key." She always locked the door if she were going to be away from the house very long. Mom said to hang the key on the chain she gave her and wear it around her neck so she wouldn't lose it. That made her feel like a little kid, but she wore it anyway, tucked away under her tee shirt where nobody could see it and laugh.

A few minutes later, Sendi walked to the park beside Pine and Gwen.

"Will we get to see your granddaughter who was on drugs?" asked Gwen.

"Sure will," said Pine. "I told her all about both of you after you met her the other day. I told her all about your major mission, Gwen."

"Good," said Gwen, looking pleased.

Pine smiled down at Sendi. "And I told her about your big old cat Monroe, Sendi. She said she wants to see him when she visits me next time."

Sendi didn't want to talk or think about Monroe right now. She didn't answer, and Pine turned back to talk to Gwen.

At the park Sendi saw all the Roscommon kids as well as the Hansen boys playing with several kids she'd never seen before. Sendi looked around at the swings and slides and tennis courts. Trees blocked out the bright sun in part of the play area. Bright flowers bloomed along the walk and in special little flower beds. Pigeons flew from the top of a wishing well and landed on the ground near several green benches.

"There's Mia," said Pine with pride as he pointed toward a girl standing beside a small pond where ducks swam. Mia's short dark hair almost touched the collar of her blue shirt. She wore Levis and cowboy boots like Pine's. She spread her hands wide as she talked to a teenage boy with a black ponytail.

Sendi frowned slightly, and then remembered that she'd run into the very same boy the day she'd learned the truth about Monroe.

Pine strode across the park, and Sendi and Gwen ran to keep up with him. "Howdy, Mia," he called and then waved.

Mia waved back, and the boy walked away in a big hurry.

Pine gave Mia a bear hug and said, "You remember Gwen and Sendi, don't you?"

"Sure do," said Mia, smiling, showing even white teeth and a dimple in her right cheek.

"Where are the others?" asked Pine, looking around.

"They stayed home," said Mia. "They said they'd be over later on after they finish their video game."

"I'll go get them later. We can't let them stay inside on such a beautiful day," said Pine.

Gwen stepped closer to Mia and said, "I'm glad you're saying no to drugs!"

Mia glanced away nervously and nodded. "Me too."

"Is that Chris, the boy you told me about?" asked Pine in a gruff voice as he motioned to the boy with the ponytail.

Mia nodded and looked ready to cry.

Pine pulled her close and held her tight. "Don't you let anybody talk you into any kind of drugs. He's wrong if he tells you the stuff he has won't get you hooked, but will make you feel better. You can get hooked on any drug, and they never make you feel better. You're clean, and you want to stay that way."

"I know, Grandpa," she said. Her voice was muffled against his chest.

Sendi wondered what it would feel like to have a grandpa. Her grandpa had divorced Momma a long time ago, and she'd never met him. He probably wouldn't hug her even if he hadn't divorced Momma. Sendi turned away and watched a duck dive under the water, and then bob back up with a piece of food in its bill.

Suddenly Gwen burst into tears. She covered her face, and her shoulders shook as she cried. A tear spotted one of the red balloons on her tee shirt.

Sendi looked helplessly at her. "Did a bee sting you, Gwen?"

"No," said Gwen, sobbing harder.

Pine knelt in front of Gwen and pulled her hands away from her face. "What's wrong, Gwenny? Tell me."

Gwen sniffed and blinked away her tears. "I never saw a drug dealer in real life. He looks like an ordinary person. He even has an ordinary name."

"Chris is a regular teenager," said Mia, sounding puzzled.

"But how can you stop them if you don't even know who to stop?" asked Gwen. "I thought you could tell the dealers from regular people. But I'd never have known by looking at him that he had anything to do with drugs! I don't think I can accomplish my major mission! I might have to give up!"

Sendi moved restlessly. She didn't

know what to say. Mia patted Gwen's arm. "Don't give up, Gwen."

Pine wiped Gwen's face with his big red hanky, and then stuffed it in his back pocket. "Gwen, you're telling kids to say no to drugs. You keep doing that. You're too small to chase down drug dealers and stop them. Someone else will have to do that, someone who's trained to spot them. But if you do your part, and others do their parts, the job will get done."

"Are you sure?" asked Gwen with a loud sniff.

Pine nodded.

Sendi glanced around the park. Her eyes widened as she saw Chris talking with two kids just a little bigger than she was. He was holding something out to them. Was it drugs? She nudged Pine. "Look," she whispered.

They all turned, and Gwen gasped.

"That boy better not tangle with me," said Pine in a sharp voice.

"Is he really trying to give them drugs?" Gwen asked in alarm.

"I bet he is," said Mia hoarsely. "He wanted me to take some. Sometimes with the little kids he gives the drugs to them without making them pay. Then the next time he makes them pay a little. Each time he makes them pay a little more until they're hooked, and they'll pay whatever the going price is."

Pine pressed his hat tighter on his head. "I'll take care of this."

"Wait," said Gwen. "I've got a good idea." She squared her shoulders and lifted her chin high. "I will get all the Roscommon kids and the Hansen boys and me and Sendi and Mia if you want to and we'll stop Chris."

Excitement bubbled inside Sendi. This sounded like fun. With all of them together they wouldn't get hurt.

She ran with Gwen to the Roscommons and Hansens. She listened as Gwen told them her plan. The other kids wanted to join in too, so Gwen let them. Sendi giggled nervously. She was glad Pine was standing beside her. He was strong and big and would help if they needed him.

"This is great!" cried Diane, bobbing up and down, her cheeks flushed with excitement.

A few minutes later, all the kids ran to where Gwen told them to go. They made a big circle around Chris and the two kids. As Sendi and the others walked closer and closer, the circle grew tighter and tighter, until it was so tight they were touching arms and even shoulders. Chris looked over at them with a scowl. The two kids looked embarrassed and glanced around for a way out.

Sendi waited for Gwen's signal, her arm raised high in the air. Suddenly Gwen shot her arm up. Everyone ran toward Chris and the two kids and yelled at the top of their voices, "NO to drugs! NO to drugs! NO to drugs! NO to drugs!"

Chris looked around in alarm, then dodged this way and that, but was blocked by kids who continued to yell, "NO to drugs!" In desperation he pushed aside Shawn Hansen and ran away as fast as he could, disappearing around a corner. The two kids just stood there with their heads down.

"We did it!" shouted Gwen, leaping high. "We did it!"

Sendi tipped back her head and laughed and clapped as hard as she could while the others did the same.

Gwen stepped up to the two kids. "Drugs will kill you," she said to them. "From now on, say no to drugs!"

"We will," they said, nodding and looking frightened.

"Job well done, Gwen," said Pine. He lifted his hat and let out a loud cowboy yell. "Job well done, kids. All of you stick together in this park, and don't let anybody come in here and try to deal drugs."

"And if you see Chris come in the park, run toward him and yell no to drugs," said Gwen. "He won't come back if we do that enough times."

Giggling, Sendi whirled around. She'd helped do something wonderful, and she felt great. Just then a black cat walked across the grass, its tail high.

The giggle died in Sendi's throat. Her arms and hands grew too weak to clap another clap. A terrible lump blocked her throat so that she couldn't shout the victory cry again.

She sank to the grass and moaned.

10

The Truth

Sendi pushed herself up off the grass and tugged on Gwen's hand. "I'm going home," she said, forcing her voice to sound normal.

"I'll see you later then," said Gwen. She turned away to talk to a couple of girls that had helped frighten Chris away.

Pine bent down to Sendi. "Are you all right?" he asked softly.

She nodded.

"We can talk if you want," he said. She shook her head.

"I have a story to tell you before you leave," he said. "Let's sit over there." He seemed so kind that she let him lead her to a bench away from the others. He sat on the bench, and she sat beside him. A tree shaded them from the bright sun.

Pine pushed his hat to the back of his head, and then took her hand in his. "Once there was a boy named Jeff who had two good friends. He was a nice boy, and his friends liked him a lot. One day Jeff met a boy named Brad who lived just down the block. Brad couldn't ever leave his yard. He had only one friend named Mark who lived right next door."

Sendi studied the hairs on the backs of Pine's fingers while she listened.

"Jeff liked Brad, but he liked Mark more. So he talked Mark into going to the park to play with him. That left Brad all alone. Jeff felt bad about that."

"I would too," said Sendi. She knew how it felt to be left all alone.

"But Jeff didn't feel bad enough to tell Mark to stay with Brad and play with him," said Pine.

"That's mean!" cried Sendi. "I would never do that!"

"Brad was all alone and lonely. He couldn't leave his yard, and now he didn't even have Mark to play with him. Jeff had Mark and his two other good friends. Brad didn't have anybody."

"That's sad," said Sendi. "Poor Brad."

Pine rubbed Sendi's hand. "If you knew someone who couldn't leave the yard, would you take away her only friend?"

"Never!" cried Sendi.

"Are you sure?" asked Pine softly.

Suddenly Sendi thought about Mrs. Yeetter and Monroe. Sendi shot a startled look at Pine. Did he know her terrible secret?

But Pine didn't say anything about her secret. He said, "Jesus loves you, Sendi. He knows all about you."

Sendi bit her bottom lip. Once again

she'd forgotten that Jesus always knew what she was doing. He knew about Monroe! Oh, it was too awful to think about! "Does Jesus love me even if I do bad things?" she whispered.

"Yes. The Bible says He does," said Pine.

Sendi locked her hands together. "What if I lie or steal?" she asked.

"Jesus still loves you," said Pine. "He doesn't want you to lie or steal, but He doesn't stop loving you."

Sendi winked back a tear. How could Jesus still love her after what she'd done? She wanted to tell Pine all about Mrs. Yeetter and Monroe, but she just couldn't.

"His love never changes," said Pine. "But something does change."

"What?" asked Sendi, barely able to sit still.

Pine tapped Sendi on the knee. "You change. You feel bad for sinning again, but feeling bad doesn't change anything."

Sendi nodded. She knew just what Pine meant. She knew she'd stolen Monroe and then lied. It was too terrible to admit even to herself. She did feel bad, but she hadn't done anything about it.

Pine said, "Jesus keeps right on loving you, but sin keeps you from feeling His love. Instead, you feel all dirty inside."

Sendi nodded. She knew that very feeling!

Pine pulled off his hat, scratched his head, and dropped his hat back in place. "But for some selfish reason, you don't want to make right the wrong you did. Because of what you've done, you've built a big wall between you and Jesus — Jesus who loves you more than your own mother loves you." Pine shook his head sadly. "And once you've put the wall up between you and Jesus, you give your enemy Satan a chance to hurt you."

"How?" asked Sendi around the hard lump in her throat.

"Because you've stepped away from Jesus, and you've walked right into the devil's territory. He makes you sad. He can steal from you, and he can hurt you."

Sendi groaned. She knew Satan was the enemy, but she never thought that he knew who she was or that he tried to make her sin.

Pine said, "The enemy will lie to you and tell you that it's all right to sin. He might even make you think that it's not sin at all."

Sendi thought about that and nodded. She'd tried to tell herself it was all right to keep Monroe just because she wanted him so badly. "What if I want to tear the wall down?" she asked. She knew the wall was the terrible secret locked in her heart. A sob rose in her throat, and she knew she couldn't live another day with the terrible wall.

Pine smiled. "The Bible says that if you tell Jesus you're sorry for your sins, He'll forgive you and make you clean again. But when you say you're sorry, you must give up the sin and not do it any more. That's what tears down the wall. Once again you're back where you belong with Jesus, and you're out of Satan's territory."

Just then Mia called to Pine. He stood up and looked down at Sendi. "Jesus loves you, Sendi. He'll help you if you just ask Him to. I have to go now, but we'll talk again later."

Sendi sat very still when Pine left. Then she jumped up and ran all the way home as fast as she could. Inside the house the great silence hit her. Mom's cologne hung in the air as well as the smell of coffee and toast. Sendi paced the kitchen, her hands locked behind her back, her head down.

"But I can't give up Monroe," she said. The sound of her voice made her jump. Inside her head she could hear Mrs. Yeetter tell about her old tomcat that had once been a tiny bit of fur that had to suck a bottle in order to stay alive.

Tears spilled down Sendi's pale cheeks. She couldn't live like this any longer! "Jesus," she said brokenly, "Jesus, I am so sorry for taking Monroe when I knew he belonged to Mrs. Yeetter! Please forgive me. And help me to do the right thing."

As she prayed, she knew the terrible wall was crumbling down. Love rose up inside her and wrapped around her. "Thank You, Jesus," she said.

After a long time, she wiped away her tears. Could she face Pine and Gwen and tell them what she'd done? Did Pine already know?

Maybe she could sneak Monroe back to Mrs. Yeetter's house and then tell Pine and Gwen that he'd gotten away.

"No!" cried Sendi, shaking her head hard. She would not step into Satan's territory again. "I won't lie again!"

Oh, but it would be much easier to sneak Monroe back and not have to face Pine and Gwen with the truth.

Sendi sank to a kitchen chair and leaned on the table. She thought of the past few days of agony. She would tell the truth even if it hurt and embarrassed her.

And what about Mrs. Yeetter? Sendi groaned. Could she tell Mrs. Yeetter the terrible truth? Maybe Diane would take Monroe home for her.

Suddenly the door burst open, and Janice rushed in, her face flushed and her eyes bright. She gripped Sendi's arms. "I just heard about what happened in the park a while ago with the drugs and the kids! I had to come see if you were okay."

"I'm fine, Mom," said Sendi with a surprised smile.

Janice sighed in relief. "Oh, Sendi, for a while I was scared that you were the one taking the drugs. You've been so moody and depressed lately. You weren't acting like yourself at all."

Sendi took a deep breath. "I did something really wrong, Mom, but it wasn't drugs."

Janice sank to a chair and stared at Sendi. "I don't know if I can handle this."

"Jesus is helping me handle it, Mom," said Sendi. "He can help you too."

"Tara at work has been telling me that," said Janice. She flipped back her blonde hair. "But we were talking about you, Sendi. What terrible thing did you do? I might as well hear it all."

Sendi leaned against the table. "Mom, I wanted a cat so bad that I took one that belonged to someone else."

Janice rubbed her forehead and stared at Sendi. "A cat? I guess you'd better tell me the whole story."

"It might take a while," said Sendi.

"That's fine," said Janice with a wave of her hand. "I told them at work that I'd stay after 5 if I didn't get back soon enough. So talk."

Sendi sank down on her chair and told all about Monroe, the cage, and Mrs. Yeetter. At first it was hard, but then it got easier.

"Oh, Sendi," said Janice when Sendi was finished, "you are a wonderful girl. I'm very proud of you."

"You are?" asked Sendi in surprise.

"I'm going to tell your dad the whole story too," said Janice with a nod.

"My dad?" asked Sendi, barely able to breathe.

Janice nodded. "Momma gave me his address, and I'm going to write to him and tell him all about you. I'm not going to be angry or bitter about him any longer." She took Sendi's hand and held it tenderly. "I have you, Sendi, my very own daughter. I don't have time to be angry or bitter. I want to enjoy my time with you. Time goes so fast, and before I know it, you'll be all grown up. If your dad doesn't want to be a part of your life, then I'm sorry for him. You're special, really, really special."

"I love you, Mom," whispered Sendi.

"I love you!" cried Janice.

Sendi ran to Mom and flung her arms around her. She was going to hug Mom even if this family didn't hug and kiss like Gwen's did.

11

Home Again

Sendi took a deep breath to steady her racing heart, and then knocked on Gwen's door. Sendi could still feel Mom's arms tight around her and her heart thudding against her ear. Mom loved her!

Gwen opened the door and smiled. "Sendi! Hi! I was just ready to come over to your place to see what was wrong."

"Can you come with me to see Pine?" asked Sendi.

"Sure," said Gwen. She called to Mrs. Lewis and told her where she was going. "That was neat what happened this morning, wasn't it?"

"I'm glad we chased Chris away from the park," said Sendi. Maybe talking to Gwen and Pine wouldn't be so hard after all.

A minute later they walked into Pine's yard. He looked up from working under the hood of his pickup. "Howdy, girls," he said, smiling as he wiped his hands on a greasy rag.

Sendi trembled. "Pine, Gwen, I have something to tell you," she said. They looked at her questioningly.

Fearfully, she told them about Monroe and Mrs. Yeetter. "I'm really sorry I lied to both of you," she said with a catch in her voice. "And I'm sorry I kept Monroe. I want to take him home now."

Gwen squeezed Sendi's hand. "I'm glad you're my very best friend."

"You're doing the right thing," said Pine, patting her shoulder. "I'm proud of you. And I'm sure glad you took care of what's been eating you."

"Thank you for the story and the talk," said Sendi. She walked to Monroe's cage. "I'll hook the leash on and walk him home."

"I'll go with you if you want," said Gwen.

"You can walk to Mrs. Yeetter's house with me, but I have to talk to her alone," said Sendi.

"You're brave," said Gwen proudly.

Just then Diane rode up on Sendi's bike. "Hi," she said. "What's going on?"

Sendi told her and Diane's face fell. "Does that mean I don't get to ride your bike anymore?"

Sendi shook her head. "You can still ride it. But not all the time. It is my bike, and I do want to ride it too."

Diane smiled. "Okay. Do you want it now?"

"No. You go ahead and ride it," said Sendi.

"Thanks." Diane pedaled away, singing at the top of her lungs.

Several minutes later, Sendi stood at Mrs. Yeetter's front door. She knew Mrs. Yeetter wouldn't answer if she knocked on her back door. Monroe was probably the only one who could use that door. Sendi had left Gwen waiting inside the corner store. Sendi's knees knocked as loudly as the knocker.

Monroe meowed and tugged at the leash.

"You're home now, Monroe," said Sendi. "I'll take off the leash and collar soon."

The door opened a crack. "What d' you want?" snapped Mrs. Yeetter.

Sendi took a deep breath. "I brought back your cat."

"My cat?" Mrs. Yeetter flung the door wide. "It *is* you!"

She scooped Monroe up, collar and leash and all. Monroe licked her all over her face, and she laughed and talked to him while tears spilled down her wrinkled cheeks. Finally she turned to Sendi. "Don't think you're going to get a reward for this," she snapped.

"I don't," said Sendi.

"It's a good thing." Suddenly Mrs. Yeetter noticed the collar and leash. "What's this all about? You trying to kill my cat?"

Sendi told Mrs. Yeetter her story. "I'm really sorry for making you sad, and I'll never try to take Monroe again."

"Monroe, huh? I never did give him a name. I didn't think he'd last long enough. I guess I could let him keep that name." Mrs. Yeetter unhooked the leash. "But he doesn't have to wear this, and I won't put a collar on him."

"But it's a law in the city," said Sendi.

"I know it is, but the last time he had on a collar, he got caught on something and tore his skin off his shoulder." Mrs. Yeetter rubbed the bare spot on Monroe's shoulder. "After that happened, I promised him I wouldn't do it to him again. He's lasted this long without a collar, and he'll last a good many more years."

"He sure is a nice cat," said Sendi, running her finger along Monroe's back.

"Well, you can't have him," snapped Mrs. Yeetter. "You go get a cat of your own. Mrs. Wells told me about free kittens when I told her my cat was gone. Go ask her about those kittens. You can always get one of your own."

"Thanks," said Sendi with a weak smile. She knew she couldn't afford to feed a cat. "Good-bye, Monroe. Good-bye, Mrs. Yeetter."

"Just hold on there," said Mrs. Yeetter. "You tell Mrs. Wells that I'll pay for cat food and for kitty litter for you until I change my mind." Mrs. Yeetter walked inside her house and slammed the door with a loud bang.

Sendi looked down at the collar and the leash in her hands. Slowly she turned and walked down the steps.

Suddenly the door burst open, and Mrs. Yeetter yelled, "Thanks for bringing back my cat. But don't you dare ever steal anything again!"

"I won't," promised Sendi. And she meant it.

"And I want you to come clean my yard for me," said Mrs. Yeetter. "That'll pay for the cat food and litter."

"Thanks!" said Sendi. "But I have to ask my mom first."

"You tell her I need your help, and that should do the trick," said Mrs. Yeetter. She slammed the door before Sendi could say anything more.

Sendi ran to the store, her eyes flashing excitedly. She stopped at the counter where Mrs. Wells and Gwen were talking. As soon as they finished, Sendi said, "Mrs. Wells, please tell me about the free kittens." Sendi knew she'd have to talk to Mom before she got one, but it was easy to talk to Mom. Mom loved her.

Mrs. Wells handed Sendi the paper advertising the free kittens. "The house is over near the park," said Mrs. Wells.

"Let's go look at them now," suggested Gwen.

"Maybe Pine would want to go with

us," said Sendi. "He might like to have a cat of his own. Let's go ask him." Sendi ran down the sidewalk beside Gwen with the ad for free kittens clutched in her hand.